better together*

*This book is best read together, grownup and kid.

a kids
book
about

a kids book about

about

IDENTITY

by Taboo

DK | Penguin Random House | **a**

A Kids Co.
Editor Jennifer Goldstein
Designer Rick DeLucco
Creative Director Rick DeLucco
Studio Manager Kenya Feldes
Sales Director Melanie Wilkins
Head of Books Jennifer Goldstein
CEO and Founder Jelani Memory

DK
Senior Production Editor Jennifer Murray
Senior Production Controller Louise Minihane
Senior Acquisitions Editor Katy Flint
Acquisitions Project Editor Sara Forster
Managing Art Editor Vicky Short
Managing Director, Licensing Mark Searle

First American edition, 2025
Published in the United States by DK Publishing, 1745 Broadway, 20th Floor,
New York, NY 10019

First published in Great Britain in 2025 by
Dorling Kindersley Limited, 20 Vauxhall Bridge Road, London SW1V 2SA
A Penguin Random House Company

The authorised representative in the EEA is
Dorling Kindersley Verlag GmbH. Arnulfstr. 124, 80636 Munich, Germany

A catalog record for this book is available from the Library of Congress.
A CIP catalogue record for this book is available from the British Library.
ISBN: 978-0-2417-4304-1

DK books are available at special discounts when purchased in bulk for sales
promotions, premiums, fund-raising, or education use. For details, contact:
DK Publishing Special Markets, 1745 Broadway, 20th Floor, New York, NY 10019
SpecialSales@dk.com

Printed and bound in China
www.dk.com
akidsco.com

FSC | MIX
Paper | Supporting
responsible forestry
FSC™ C018179

This book was made with Forest
Stewardship Council™ certified
paper – one small step in DK's
commitment to a sustainable future.
Learn more at **www.dk.com/uk/
information/sustainability**

This book is dedicated to my kids:
Josh, Jalen, Journey, and Jett Gomez.

Intro
for grownups

Who are you? Who am I? A lot of the time, when we hear this, we simply answer with our names, but we're so much more than that! When you describe yourself to others or think about who you are, the words collect into descriptions that form what we call our identity.

But no matter how empowering discovering who we are is, it's important to remember that our identities describe us but don't define us. Some identities we are born with and some we choose, but we're the ones that give them power and meaning.

This is a book about my journey in discovering and learning about who I am and why I'm in this beautiful world. The funny thing is, it changes as we live each day. I hope this book helps you learn how to recognize the things that make you, you.

WHO ARE YOU?

When you hear that question,
do you answer with your name?

Or where you are from?

Or where your parents or
grandparents were born?

With what you love?

With your superpower?

You can be so many
different things.

But did you know that
any way you answer,
"Who are you?"
is part of your...

IDENTITY.

Identity is who you are, the way you think about yourself, and the things you choose to describe yourself.

It's a combination of all the things that make you unique and special.

My name is
JIMMY GOMEZ.

But you probably
know me as **TABOO**.

My friends and
relatives call me **TAB**.

And when I'm in my zone
and ready to rock the stage...

I AM
TABOO
NAWASHA.

I have so many names because I'm so many things!

I'm a dancer, an MC,* and a founding member of the **BLACK EYED PEAS.**

*In hip hop culture, an MC is another way to say a rapper. I prefer to be called an MC.

But most of the time,

I'm just Jaymie's **HUSBAND**.

I'm also **DAD** to my kids.

I'm even a **COLLECTOR**
of toys and sneakers.

These are all part of my identity.

But I haven't always
been all of these things.

I grew up in **EAST LA.***

*LA stands for Los Angeles, a city in California.

I'm of **NATIVE** and **MEXICAN** descent.

My grandmother represents my **NATIVE** heritage, while my **MEXICAN** heritage comes from my grandfather.

Nanny is what we
called my grandmother.

She loved her family
and taught us the ways
of our people, which were
handed down to her.

That's part of
my identity too.

Where I grew up in California, just about everyone has **INDIGENOUS** roots, which can be traced back to Mexico.

Those roots are another part of my identity.

We are
MEXICAN AMERICAN
people and we call ourselves
CHICANOS.

Most people in East LA speak Spanglish, which is a combination of English and Spanish, and life there is a beautiful mosaic of

MEXICAN and

AMERICAN

traditions, food, and music.

My Nanny danced to express herself, and when I dance, I feel the heartbeat and the drum of my ancestors pounding inside me.

That's part of my **IDENTITY.**

She believed in me and would set me up like a real star, calling out, "From Los Angeles, California, give it up for..."

"JIMMY

And I would be rocking at her house

GOMEZ!"
like I was performing for 80,000 people.

I didn't grow up with my grandfather or my dad, so I learned about my **MEXICAN** heritage from the people around me.

Nanny gave me the gift of becoming a **PERFORMER** and a **DANCER**, and now that's part of my identity—who I am.

Identity is about who you are.

BUT NONE OF US ARE JUST 1 THING.

Some parts of our identity we're born with.

And some we choose.

Parts of our identity
can be obvious to others.

And other parts might be

HIDDEN.

Others can help you along
your journey to discover

WHO YOU ARE,

WHAT YOU LOVE,

and **WHAT'S TRUE ABOUT YOU.**

But you don't have to keep every name, word, or identity other people might label you with.

One of the things I want you to know about **YOUR** identity is...

YOU GET TO DECIDE WHAT IT MEANS TO YOU.

Because identity is all about

BEING
WHO YO

OU ARE.

And not just that—it's also about **KNOWING** who you are.

Identity can be about

YOUR RACE,

YOUR GENDER,

YOUR HOMETOWN,

YOUR SCHOOL,

YOUR FAITH,

WHAT YOU'VE LOST,

or **WHAT YOU'VE GAINED.**

As a dancer and an MC,
I get to travel around the
world and do what I love.

I get to show who I am to lots
of people and I represent my
culture with how I dress.

Identity can be things
like that too.

I like to rock a **TURQUOISE PIECE** or a lil' bit of Native bling to express my **NATIVE ROOTS** and feel like my ancestors are with me.

There's no greater
feeling than getting to be

Y O

ou.

And as you grow up, you'll keep discovering new parts of yourself.

NEW WAYS YOU IDENTIFY.

Some of them might have
been there all along.

Some might start like a
seed that grows over time,
getting bigger as you get older.

But identity isn't just formed by **EASY** or **FUN** things— part of what shapes you is the **CHALLENGES** you've faced.

These challenges are like big, scary giants, towering over you and trying to take you down.

I like to call it

"FIGH
GIA

TING
NTS."

Because even though they
may seem impossible to beat,
we have the strength to fight back.

Back in 2014,
I found out I had cancer.

That was one of
the biggest **GIANTS**
I ever had to **FIGHT**.

I didn't know what to do—but
my wife, kids, and family did.

Without them, I don't
think I would've had the
strength to beat it.

The doctor's medicine worked to stop the cancer, but it made my body weak, and my spirit—my true identity—even weaker.

During my journey of healing:

I RECONNECTED with my Native roots.

I ATE FOODS that gave my body the energy it needed.

I MEDITATED AND LISTENED to my heart.

I SPENT TIME outdoors and became one with the earth.

AND I FELT DEEP JOY to be with my family and friends who love me.

Now my identity includes

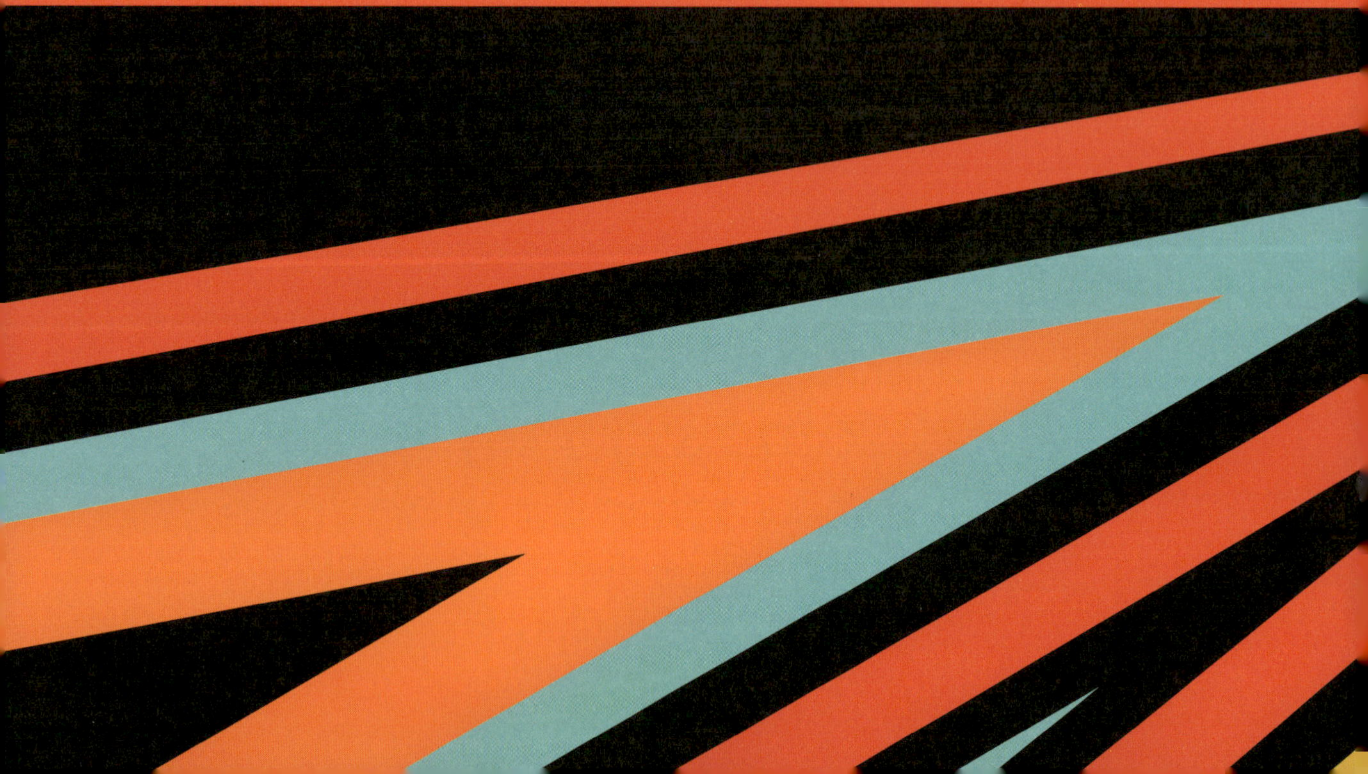

being a **CANCER SURVIVOR,**

an advocate for
**INDIGENOUS
COMMUNITIES,**

and someone who honors
MY WHOLE SELF—

MEXICAN and **NATIVE.**

So now that you know a bit more about me, who I am, and my identity...

WHO ARE YOU?

Outro
for grownups

Lyrics from the original song *Fighting Giants* by **Taboo**.

This is a book about identity and how I fight giants.

Yeah, let me tell you about a strong man overcoming all the things that stand in the way of what he's fighting for, but he just keeps pushing till he finds that cure for hatred, complications, those that can't see that love's the greatest thing that we all could share, if we just stand up today, we all got a voice to say!

I just want to say to you it's all right.

So, I'm gonna keep on fighting giants—no matter how big, how small, how tall—just give me one good reason I can't make them fall. You see, everything you put between us, standing outside your fortress walls, and I'm gonna keep on fighting giants till I make them fall.

Let me tell you about a world I know, where the people got so much soul, doesn't matter if you're big or small. You can be yourself if you just stand tall. Stand up! Don't you ever let 'em get you down. No turning back 'cause it's your time now. Let your sun shine bright. It will be just right today.

We all got a voice to say, I just want to say to you it's all right.

Down, down, down. Stand up!

Made to empower.

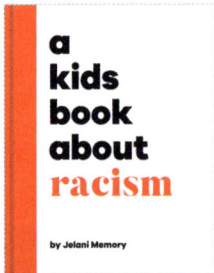

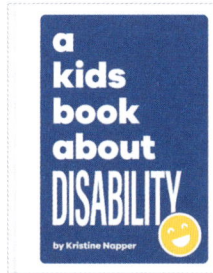

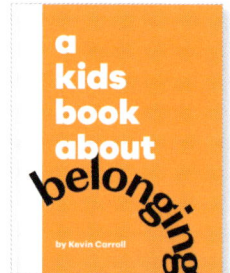

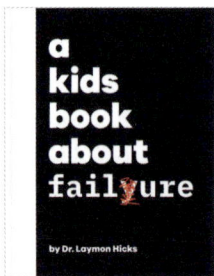

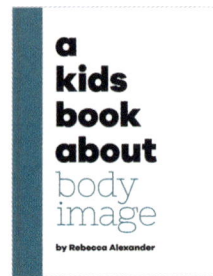

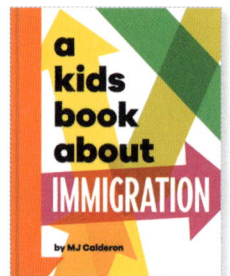

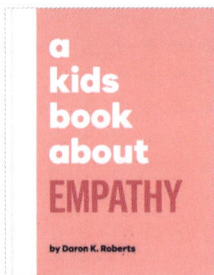

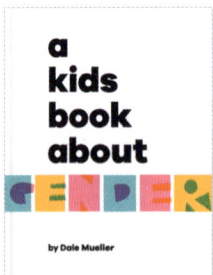

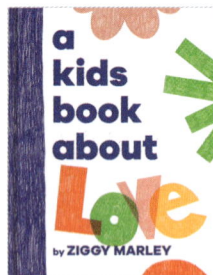

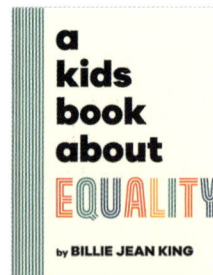

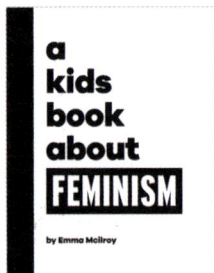

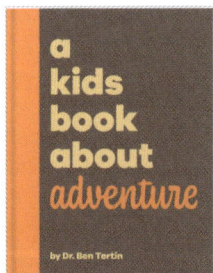

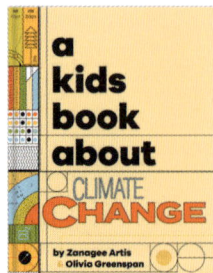

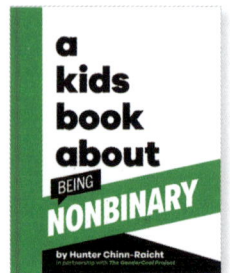

a kids book about **racism**
by Jelani Memory

a kids book about ANXIETY
by Ross Szabo

a kids book about DISABILITY
by Kristine Napper

a kids book about IMAGINATION
by LEVAR BURTON

a kids book about belonging
by Kevin Carroll

a kids book about failyure
by Dr. Laymon Hicks

a kids book about GRATITUDE
by Ben Kenyon

a kids book about LIFE ONLINE
by Dave S. Anderson & Blake Fleischacker

a kids book about body image
by Rebecca Alexander

a kids book about IMMIGRATION
by MJ Calderon

a kids book about EMPATHY
by Daron K. Roberts

a kids book about GENDER
by Dale Mueller

a kids book about Love
by ZIGGY MARLEY

a kids book about EQUALITY
by BILLIE JEAN KING

a kids book about MONEY
by Adam Stramwasser

a kids book about FEMINISM
by Emma McIlroy

a kids book about adventure
by Dr. Ben Tertin

a kids book about CLIMATE CHANGE
by Zanagee Artis & Olivia Greenspan

a kids book about CONFIDENCE
by Joy Cho

a kids book about BEING NONBINARY
by Hunter Chinn-Raicht
in partnership with The GenderCool Project

Discover more at akidsco.com